MEET TRICKY COYOTE!

Other Books by Gretchen Will Mayo

That Tricky Coyote

Earthmaker's Tales
North American Indian Stories About Earth Happenings

Star Tales
North American Indian Stories About the Stars

Books Illustrated by Gretchen Will Mayo

Whale Brother

MEET TRICKY COYOTE!

Retold and Illustrated by
Gretchen Will Mayo

WALKER AND COMPANY **NEW YORK**

PEOPLE IMAGINE COYOTE IN MANY WAYS. SOME SAY COYOTE SHIMMERS. THIS IS THE VISION THAT GREW IN THE ARTIST'S MIND AS SHE GOT TO KNOW COYOTE AND DREW THE PICTURES FOR THIS BOOK.

First published in the United States of America in 1993 by Walker Publishing Company, Inc.
Published simultaneously in Canada by Thomas Allen & Son Canada, Limited, Markham, Ontario

Library of Congress Cataloging-in-Publication Data
Mayo, Gretchen.
Meet tricky Coyote! / retold by Gretchen Will Mayo.
p.   cm.
Includes bibliographical references.
Summary: A collection of legends about the cunning trickster Coyote, taken from a variety of Native American sources.
ISBN 0-8027-8198-5. —ISBN 0-8027-8199-3 (R)
1. Coyote (Legendary character)   2. Indians of North America—Legends.   [1. Coyote (Legendary character)   2. Indians of North America—Legends.]   I. Title.
E98.F6M3425   1993
398.24'52974442—dc20   92-12424
                         CIP
                         AC

The art was prepared in opaque acrylic paints on paper.

Book Design by Georg Brewer

Printed in Hong Kong
10 9 8 7 6 5 4 3 2 1

FOR MY SISTER, JULIE, AND MY BROTHERS, MARK, KEMP, AND PETE, WHO GATHERED THEIR OWN BAG OF TRICKS WHEN WE WERE KIDS.

CONTENTS

ACKNOWLEDGMENTS

In researching the Coyote stories and pictures, I was helped by many people and institutions. I offer thanks and admiration to Dr. Jay Miller, D'Arcy McNickle Center for the History of the American Indian, the Newberry Library, Chicago; the Milwaukee Public Museum and its library staff (especially Judy Turner); the State Historical Society of Colorado; the Marquette University Library Archives Department; the University of Wisconsin for use of its library; Joseph Bruchac, Abenaki storyteller and author; Dr. Kimberly Blaeser; and Dr. Alice B. Kehoe, anthropologist and author of *North American Indians: A Comprehensive Account*, Prentice-Hall, Inc., 1981.

I am indebted to Margaret Jensen, who read the manuscript in progress, for sharing her enthusiasm for and expertise in books for the early reader.

Meet Tricky Coyote!

Meet Tricky Coyote!
He thinks he can do anything.
It's true, Coyote did some good things.
He gave us fire. He made the mountains.
He put the stars in the sky.
Such important work!
You would think Coyote could behave.
But he doesn't.
He is greedy.
He is silly.
He cheats.
He brags.
What a mischief-maker!
When will you learn, Coyote?

Tricky Coyote

Coyote was walking along when a man came down the road. The man was riding a fine horse. He was dressed in fancy clothes. He wore a fancy hat. When the man saw Coyote, he stopped.

"Well, well, well!" said the man. "Are you the famous Coyote?"

"That's me!" answered Coyote.

The man grinned. "I've heard all about you, Coyote," said Fancy Man. "I hear you are very tricky."

"You're so right!" bragged Coyote.

"I'll bet you can't trick me," said Fancy Man. "I'm too smart. I'm tricky, too. Let's have a contest. Let's see who can do the best trick."

"Oh, no!" said Coyote. "You will win."

"Why are you so sure?" asked Fancy Man.

"Because I need my bag of tricks, but I left it at home," Coyote replied.

"Well, go get the bag. Get it right now. Then we can have a contest," said Fancy Man.

"No way!" cried Coyote. "My house is far, far away. It will take a long time to get there. I will be too tired."

The man gave Coyote a sly look. "I think you are afraid of a contest," said the man. "I think you are afraid I will win."

"Okay! Okay! I'll go get my bag of tricks," Coyote answered. "But you will have to let me ride your horse."

So Fancy Man slipped off his horse. He gave his horse to Coyote, but the horse jumped away.

"My horse doesn't like you," said Fancy Man. "He doesn't want you to ride."

"Maybe we could trick the horse," said Coyote. "If I wear your shirt, maybe the horse will think I am you."

"Yes, yes!" cried the man. "Then the horse will let you ride!" Fancy Man took off his fancy shirt. He gave it to Coyote.

"You better give me your pants, too," Coyote said. "Give me your pants, just to make sure the horse will like me."

2

"Good idea!" cried Fancy Man. He gave Coyote his fancy pants.

Then Coyote jumped up on the man's horse. Coyote started to ride away. But he stopped.

"Ooooh! The sun is too hot," said Coyote. "It will burn my head. I can't go on."

Fancy Man ran up to Coyote. "Here, Coyote! Take my hat. My hat will keep the sun away. Then you can get your bag of tricks." He gave Coyote his fancy hat.

Coyote put on the fancy hat. "Get going!" Coyote said to the fancy horse.

Fancy Man shouted, "Hurry back for the contest, Coyote! Hurry back with your bag of tricks!"

Coyote looked back and laughed. "Who needs a bag of tricks?" he yelled. "I have your fancy hat. I have your fancy shirt and fancy pants. I am riding your fancy horse. What do *you* have, Fancy Man?"

"Hey! Come back here, Coyote!" shouted the man. "I've been tricked!" But fancy Coyote had ridden away.

"Tricky Coyote" is the Comanche version of a popular tale. Like many American Indian stories, this one has grown and changed as it was passed from group to group. It was recorded in Wyoming in 1909. The ancestors of today's Comanches were nomadic hunters of the central plains.

BURRRRRRRRRRP!

Fox was eating when Coyote came along.

"What are you eating?" asked Coyote.

"Have some," answered Fox.

Coyote took a taste. "That's good!" he said, licking his lips. "What is it?"

"The people call it cheese. Want some more?"

"You bet!" said Coyote.

"Then follow me!" Fox took Coyote to a hole in the ground. Fox crawled in and under. He crawled up the hole and into a building. "Crawl in, Coyote!" Fox called from inside.

Coyote was bigger than Fox. He squeezed in. He squashed under. He pushed up.

Coyote looked around inside the building. "Hey! There's lots of cheese here!" cried Coyote.

"Take some and run," Fox said.

"But I want to eat now," Coyote answered. He took a little bite. "Yum!" He took a big bite. "Yum, yum!"

"Better hurry," called Fox.

Coyote didn't hurry. He ate and ate and ate.

"Don't eat too much," said Fox.

"Why not? This is good!" Coyote answered. "Burp! Burrrrp!" said fat Coyote and fat Coyote fell over. "Burrrrrrrrp!"

"Who's making all that noise in there?" someone shouted. Then someone with a big broom opened the door.

"Run!" cried Fox. He jumped back in the hole, he crawled under, and pushed outside again. "Made it!" puffed Fox. He ran away fast. But where was Coyote?

Coyote was still inside. Coyote was in *big* trouble.

"Get out of here!" someone with a broom yelled at Coyote. "Get out!"

Coyote ran to the hole. Thumpa, thumpa, thumpa, thumpa.

Fat Coyote tried to squeeze in the hole. Uuuuuuumph! Ooooooph! Ummmmmmph!

Then Coyote yelled, "Help, Fox! Help! I'm stuck!"

But no one could help Coyote now.

"Thief! Thief!" someone cried. Someone hit Coyote's tail with the broom—womp, womp, womp!

"Ouch!" cried Coyote. He squeezed. He pushed. He pulled himself outside.

Safe at last! "I made it!" puffed Coyote. He ran away fast. But where was Fox?

Fox was hiding in the bushes and watching. "Hee, hee, hee!" laughed Fox.

"What's so funny?" cried Coyote.

"You are," answered Fox. "You are so fat. You are so dirty. And your coat is so tight."

"Burrrrrrrp! Yes, but I am full of good food!" laughed Coyote. "Burrrrrrrp!"

A group of Salishan people who lived along the Thompson River in Canada just north of the Washington State border had many stories about Fox and Coyote. Their version of "Burrrrrrrrrrp!" reflects their contact with Europeans. It was recorded in 1916.

What Is in Mole's Sack?

Coyote was walking along. "There is Mole's tunnel!" said Coyote. He went over to look.

Scritch, scrape, scrape. Mole was busy.

"Working hard, Mole?" called Coyote.

"Yup!" Mole scraped some more.

Coyote found a tree and sat down to watch Mole. Coyote thought, "I'm so smart. I can rest in the shade. No hard work for me!"

Mole ran in and out of his house. He carried a little sack on his back.

"Mole, why are you working so hard?" Coyote called. He leaned against the tree.

"Busy cleaning," answered Mole. He scraped some more.

Coyote stared at Mole's sack. "Why is Mole carrying that sack?" Coyote wondered. "What does he have in it?"

Coyote called out, "Mole, you must have something good in your sack."

"Nope," said Mole.

Coyote didn't believe him. Coyote thought, "If I had

something good in a sack, I would keep it just for me. I'll bet Mole doesn't want to share."

Coyote called sweetly, "Let me look in your sack."

"Nope," said Mole.

"Just a little peek," begged Coyote. "I'll just open the sack a little bit."

"Don't," Mole said.

Coyote jumped up. He walked over to Mole. "I know. You want to keep the sack just for you."

"Nope," answered Mole.

"Well, I'm bigger," Coyote yelled at Mole. "You won't let me take a look, so I'll take the whole thing!" And he did. Coyote grabbed Mole's sack and ran back down the road. He hid behind a rock. He smiled a little smile. Then he opened the sack.

"Eeeeeeeeee, no!" he cried. Zit-zit-zit-zit-zit! Out leaped a crowd of fleas. They jumped all over Coyote.

"Go away!" Coyote yelled. "Go away!" He slap-slap-slapped. He hopped. He rolled in the dirt. But the fleas hung on to Coyote. They liked his ears. They liked his back. They liked this big Coyote.

Coyote ran back to Mole's tunnel. "Mole!" he cried. "Take back your fleas. Take them back!"

But Mole ran away. He ran into his house and would not come out.

Coyote can't rest in the shade now. Scratch! Scratch! Scratch! Coyote is busy all the time. Scratching fleas is hard work.

"What Is in Mole's Sack?" is adapted from a story told in 1899 by a Maidu storyteller. Many Maidu still live in the mountain valleys west of the Sierra Range in Northern California. Their ancestors lived and hunted there hundreds of years ago.

WHAT'S SO GREAT ABOUT CRANES?

Coyote was walking beside the river when the water began to rise.

Splash, splash, splash! Suddenly Coyote's feet were wet. Splash, splash, splash! The river spilled over his feet. It covered the ground all around.

"Hey!" yelled Coyote. "It's a flood!"

Coyote waded over to a tree. He grabbed a branch and climbed up.

"Wow! Look at all that water!" said Coyote. "It's rising higher and higher. Guess I'm stuck here until the water goes down." Wet Coyote sat on the branch and watched the water below. He sat and waited, sat and waited. Ho-hum.

Then suddenly Crane flew out of the sky. Her wide wings swept her over the water to a tree near Coyote. Crane settled in the tree and watched the flood, too.

Coyote thought, "If I had wings like Crane, I sure wouldn't stick around here."

All at once, Coyote heard singing. It was Crane. "The water is going down," she sang.

"Is she crazy?" said Coyote. "Water is all around here. It still looks like a flood to me."

Then Crane stretched out one long leg. She stretched her leg and reached her foot deep into the water. "The water is going down," she sang. Then she lifted some mud from the bottom.

"How did she do that?" thought Coyote. "How did Crane lift that mud out of the flood?"

Crane stretched her long leg out again and lifted some more

mud. "Yes, the water is going down," she sang. "The water is going down." Each time she said "down" Crane lifted some mud from the water.

"How did you do that?" called Coyote.

"We cranes have long legs," answered Crane. "I can touch the bottom. If you were a crane, you could touch bottom."

Coyote looked at the water below. "What's so great about cranes? I can touch the bottom, too!" muttered Coyote. "And I can sing better than she can!" Then, just like Crane, Coyote sang, "The water is going down." And just like Crane, Coyote stretched his leg down from the tree. But Coyote's leg was short. Coyote's paw couldn't even reach the water.

Coyote pulled back his short leg. He pulled it back fast so Crane couldn't see. Coyote peeked over at Crane.

Crane had stretched out her long leg again. "See, the water is going down," she sang. And she showed Coyote some more mud. "The water is going down."

"Who cares!" grumbled Coyote.

"I do," answered Crane. "The water is going down, so now I can walk in the water." Crane reached out her two long legs and stepped into the water. "If you were a crane, you could walk in the water now, too."

"Who says I can't walk in the water?" yelled Coyote. "Coyotes can do anything a crane can do." Coyote jumped out of the tree. He splashed into the water. But the water was high. It was higher than Coyote. He sank like a stone.

"Hey! Glub, glub, glub, glub," said Coyote. At last his feet touched the bottom. But Coyote's nose did not reach the top.

"Glub, glub, glub." Coyote pushed his nose up, out of the water. Now his feet could not touch the bottom. Swish! The flood twirled Coyote around.

"Hey! I can't stop!" yelled Coyote. "Get me out of here! Help!"

Then Crane picked up Coyote. She lifted him out of the water. She carried him to a dry spot and dropped him there.

"I suppose I should thank you for saving me," said Coyote.

"You should," said Crane.

"But I won't," said Coyote.

"Why not?" asked Crane.

"Because, it's your fault that I jumped out of the tree. It's your fault that I almost drowned," answered Coyote.

"My fault?" cried Crane.

"Sure!" said Coyote. "Your legs are too long."

"That doesn't make any sense," said Crane.

"Yes, it does," Coyote answered. "If your legs were the right size, like mine, none of this would have happened."

"Coyote, you are weird." Crane sighed.

"What's So Great About Cranes?" is a flood story told and recorded in 1910 by one of the Desert People, Juan Dolores, who was a scholar of the Papago, or Tohona O'odham, language. Although they lived in the Sonoran Desert in Arizona, Juan Dolores and his relatives might have experienced flash floods when rain or snow drained from the mountaintops and spilled beyond the riverbeds.

Go Away, Cloud!

Coyote was walking along when a big shadow darkened his path. He looked up and saw one big cloud. He could not see the sun.

"Move along, Cloud!" called Coyote. "I like the sun to shine on me. I like the sun to make me warm."

But the big cloud did not hurry.

Coyote watched and thought, "Cloud is lazy. He crawls like Turtle. He creeps like Snail. I will never see the sun today. How can I make Cloud move faster?"

Then Coyote had an idea. He called to Cloud, "I dare you to race me, Cloud. Race me to the edge of the earth."

Cloud rolled over in the sky. "Why should I race?" asked Cloud. "I don't like to hurry. I don't like to rush."

Coyote called back, "Racing is fun if you win."

22

"If I win, what will you give me?" asked Cloud. "You must give me something nice."

Coyote thought again. "Clouds are slow, but Coyotes are fast," he said to himself. "We will race. Cloud will hurry. But I will win." Then Coyote smiled as he thought, "When I win, I won't have to give Cloud anything!"

So Coyote looked up and promised Cloud, "If you win, you can have any prize. What prize do you want?"

"I want to make big storms. If I win, I will rumble and roar and blow on the land," Cloud answered.

"Okay," Coyote agreed. "If you win the race, you can rumble

and roar and blow anytime. You can turn black and puff up and fill the sky."

Then Coyote smiled again. "But if I win, Cloud, you must go away and hide. You must stay away so I can see the sun. I like the sun to shine on me. I like the sun to make me warm."

So Coyote and Cloud began their race.

Coyote ran as fast as he could. He ran and ran to get ahead. Then Coyote saw the sun again. "Where is Cloud's big shadow?" wondered Coyote. "Cloud must be far behind." He looked back to see.

There was Cloud, far behind in the big blue sky. He crawled like Turtle. He crept like Snail. But as he moved along, Cloud sent down a gentle rain. Thirsty plants lifted their leaves. Blossoms unfolded. Fruits grew round.

Coyote turned around. "Wow! Look at all that good food!" cried Coyote. "I'm thirsty. I'm hungry. And I'm faster than Cloud. I can stop for just a little while. I can eat just a little bit."

Coyote ran back under Cloud's big shadow. He grabbed some fruit and gobbled it up. "Yum, yum," said Coyote. "I see so many things to eat." He did not see Cloud's shadow go away.

The sun beamed down on Coyote while he ate and ate. Greedy Coyote stuffed his mouth and forgot all about Cloud. So Cloud drifted alone to the end of the earth.

"Uh-oh! Where is Cloud?" thought Coyote at last. He stopped munching. He dropped the fruit. Then Coyote shot like an arrow to catch up with Cloud.

But Coyote was too late. He found Cloud waiting for him at the edge of the earth. "Where have you been, Coyote?" asked Cloud.

"Never mind!" pouted Coyote. Coyote was not the winner, so he had to keep his promise to Cloud.

Now Cloud and all of Cloud's children and grandchildren float wherever they wish in the big, blue sky. Sometimes they send down a gentle rain. Then flowers and berries and round

fruits grow. But other times they turn black and puff up and fill the sky. They rumble and roar and blow on the land. All because Coyote was greedy.

In northern California, along the Pit River and between high mountains, lies the traditional homeland of the Achumawi. In 1900 two Achumawi, Charley Green and a storyteller known as "Old Wool," told the story of a race between Cloud and Coyote that brought year-round storms to the earth. "Go Away, Cloud!" is based on their tale.

WHO IS COYOTE?

While it can become overly romanticized, Indians favor circles over squares and webs over grids. The world of the Indian has a roundness and a closeness that reflect important values. Within every circle there is a center that holds everything together. For the village, the center was usually the community hall or the house of the leader. On tribal lands, the center was often a sacred mountain, spring, or special place. In the stories of Native American tribes living in Western North America, Coyote became another such center.

Coyote was a complex character who stood at the center of many things. Because he was at the very middle, Coyote could see and do anything in any direction, whether it was for good or bad, to hurt or to help. Some stories have Coyote holding up the sky or changing the temperament of an entire species of animal. Often hills and trees are located where they are because of something Coyote did or did not do that changed the world forever.

Coyote was so important you would think that he knew how to behave, or would at least learn. But as you see, he did not. As often as not, Coyote set a bad example and sometimes a horrible one. Only too rarely, he managed to do something nice, although this was almost never by deliberate design. Even so, people act the way they do now because of something that Coyote did during the time that the world was forming.

In this way Coyote was and is a fixture of the life and landscape of Native America. While other parts of the Americas had other animals who served a similar role, such as Rabbit in the East and Raven along the coasts of the northern Pacific, only Coyote was truly an American original. Coyote owes his importance both to the wily ways of a real coyote and to the intimate ties that humans and canines have had for eons. What makes Coyote so distinctly American, moreover, is the manner in which this character is cast in these stories.

Gretchen Will Mayo has taken care to tailor her selections to a young audience and has wisely limited the panoramic perspective that got Coyote into so much trouble over the generations. Here he is wise and foolish and childish, but nevertheless entertaining. He lives as much in the world of today as in the world of our ancestors. Coyote's stories teach us the importance of sustaining the diversity of life on earth for the benefit of the global community in which Coyote is both first citizen and last resort.

Jay Miller, Ph.D.,
D'Arcy McNickle Center for the History of the American Indian,
The Newberry Library, Chicago

SOURCES

Usually scholars in the fields of anthropology and ethnology were the first to record tales told by American Indian storytellers. It should always be remembered, however, that the stories belong to the creative Indians who told them. We thank and honor those Native Americans who shared their stories for the following reporters and publications:

Dixon, Roland B. "Some Coyote Stories from the Maidu Indians." *Journal of American Folklore* 13: 267–70.

"Achomawi and Alsugewi Tales." *Journal of American Folklore* 21: 159–77.

Kroeber, Henriette Rothschild. "Papago Coyote Tales." *Journal of American Folklore* 22: 34–42.

Lowie, Robert H., and St. Clair II, H. H. "Shoshoni and Comanche Tales." *Journal of American Folklore* 22: 265–82.

Teit, James A. "European Tales from the Upper Thompson Indians." *Journal of American Folklore* 29: 301–29.

These additional resources were used for background information:

Coffer, William. *Where Is the Eagle?* New York: Van Nostrand Reinhold and Company, 1981.

Lopez, Barry Holstun. *Giving Birth to Thunder, Sleeping with His Daughter*. New York: Avon Books, 1977.

Miller, Jay. Introduction and Notes to *Coyote Stories*. Lincoln: University of Nebraska Press, First Bison Book Printing, 1990.

Mourning Dove. *Coyote Stories*. Lincoln: University of Nebraska Press, First Bison Book Printing, 1990.

Radin, Paul. *The Trickster, A Study in American Indian Mythology*. London: Routledge and Kegan Paul, 1956.

Tedlock, Barbara. *The Clown's Way—Teachings from the American Earth*. New York: Liveright Press, 1975.

Tedlock, Dennis. *The Spoken Word and the Work of Interpretation*. Philadelphia: University of Pennsylvania Press, 1983.